THIS BOOK BELONGS TO

DIANE GOODE

THE DINOSAUR'S

A RETELLING OF THE HANS CHRISTIAN ANDERSEN TALE

THE BLUE SKY PRESS • AN IMPRINT OF SCHOLASTIC INC. • NEW YORK

ONCE UPON A TIME, THERE LIVED AN EMPEROR WHO WAS SO FOND OF NEW CLOTHES that he spent all his money on them. He had a different coat for every hour of the day, and whenever he was needed, he could always be found in his dressing room.

One day, two swindlers came to the great city where the Emperor lived. Knowing the Emperor's fondness for clothes, they pretended to be weavers and said they could make the finest cloth ever seen. Not only was it beautiful, but it was magical: The clothing made from this cloth was invisible to anyone who was either hopelessly stupid or else unfit for his job.

"What splendid clothes!" thought the Emperor. "If I wear them, I can find out who is wise and who should be fired from his job. Yes, I must have the cloth woven for me!" So he paid the swindlers a large sum of money to begin their work at once.

The swindlers set up a loom, but they used no thread on their shuttles. They pretended to work at their empty loom far into the night.

After a few days, the Emperor was eager to know how the cloth was coming along. "I shall send my faithful old minister. He is very smart, and no one is better at his job. Therefore he will be the best judge of the cloth."

So the faithful old minister went to the hall where the swindlers sat working at the empty loom.

The old minister looked closely at the loom. "Heaven help me!" he thought. "Why, I can't see any cloth at all!" He stepped closer. "Can I be stupid? Am I unfit for my job? If the Emperor finds out, he will surely fire me!"

"Oh, it is beautiful," the old minister said. "Charming! I shall tell the Emperor all about it."

And the old minister listened carefully as the swindlers described the colors and patterns so he could repeat them to the Emperor—and he did.

Soon the Emperor sent a
second faithful minister to see
when the new clothes would be ready.

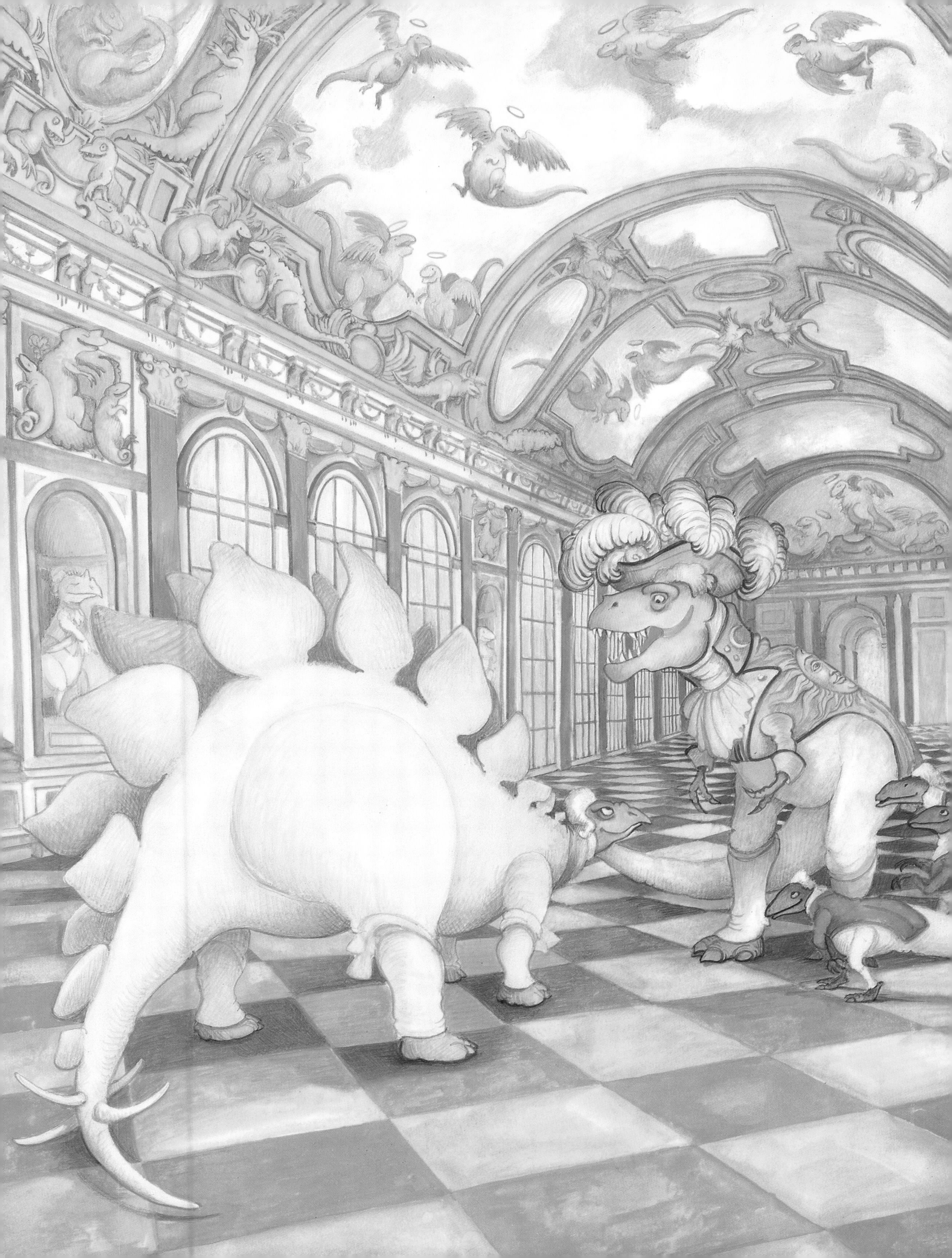

The second minister looked and looked, but he could see no cloth on the loom.

"Isn't it splendid?" asked the swindlers.

"Now, I *know* I am not stupid," thought the minister. "So it must be that I am unfit for my job. I must not let anyone find out!"

So he praised the cloth he did not see.

"Yes," he told the Emperor, "it is absolutely delightful!"

Soon everyone in town
was talking about the splendid new cloth.

At last, the Emperor, accompanied by the two faithful ministers and his courtiers, went to visit the swindlers.

"Isn't it beautiful, Your Majesty?" asked the ministers, pointing to the empty loom, for they thought all the others could see the cloth.

"What's this?" thought the Emperor. "I see nothing at all! Am I stupid? Am I unfit to be Emperor? Why, this is terrible!"

So he pretended to see the cloth and said, “Oh, it is very fine. It has my highest approval!”

“Yes, it is very fine! Delightful! Superb!” exclaimed all the courtiers, though they saw nothing at all. And they told the Emperor that he should wear a suit of clothes made from this wonderful cloth at the next great procession.

The night before the procession, the swindlers worked all night. They wanted everyone to see how anxious they were to finish the Emperor's new clothes. They pretended to take the cloth down from the loom. They cut the air with enormous scissors. They sewed with threadless needles. And at last they proclaimed, "The Emperor's new clothes are ready!"

When it was time for the Emperor to dress, the swindlers held up their empty arms. "See, Your Majesty," they exclaimed, "your beautiful new clothes are as light as cobwebs!"

Then the swindlers pretended to give him trousers, a coat, and robes, and they pretended to tie on a train. The Emperor turned round and round in front of the mirror as if he were admiring his new suit.

"How well His Majesty looks! What a fit! They're the most splendid clothes!" everyone declared.

The chamberlains, who were supposed to carry the Emperor's train, stooped and pretended to lift it. Then they walked along with their empty hands in the air.

And so the Emperor marched in his procession, and all who saw him cried out, “Look at the Emperor’s beautiful new clothes. What a magnificent train! What a cloak!”

They all pretended to see the garments that were not there, for they did not dare to appear stupid. None of the Emperor's clothes had ever been so successful.

Then, suddenly, a small child cried out, "But the Emperor has nothing on!"

Those who heard the child began to whisper, and soon the whispers spread throughout the crowd: "He has nothing on—an innocent child says the Emperor has nothing on!"

"The Emperor isn't wearing any clothes!" everyone cried at last.

And the Emperor stiffened, for he knew it was true. "Nonetheless," he thought, "the procession must go on."

And so he continued to walk, holding himself more proudly than ever—while the chamberlains held up a train made of cloth that had never been there at all.

A NOTE ABOUT THIS BOOK

The delightfully witty tale "The Emperor's New Clothes" was written by Danish writer Hans Christian Andersen (1805–1875). Hundreds of versions have been published throughout the world, and theatrical, musical, and film adaptations have entertained audiences for more than a century.

Andersen's humorous story has always been the favorite tale of Caldecott Honor illustrator Diane Goode, and she has wanted to illustrate a picture-book adaptation of it for many years. The primary setting of this book, the palace of Versailles, has been in her consciousness since she was a little girl. Her mother was French, and Goode spent her summers in France. "Versailles is overwhelming," she explains. "It was the home of France's last king, and an aristocracy that was on its way to extinction. Over the years, I have gone back to revisit it. I have picnicked in the woods and along the canal; I have wandered through the long corridors, time and again. It is endlessly fascinating to me. Never did I imagine I would be bringing it to children as a playful parody."

During the late eighteenth century, the passion for fashion was so intense that it reached extremes in both luxury and imagination that would never be known again. "Dressing the dinosaurs, giving them personalities, homes of their own, creating the Emperor's costumes embroidered with children's stories—all of it was great fun," Goode relates. The characters are all based on real dinosaurs. Beneath the powdered wigs and period costumes, young readers who are interested will recognize the Emperor as a *Tyrannosaurus rex*, the small weaver as a *Proceratosaurus*, the first minister as an *Iguanodon*, and the second minister as a *Stegosaurus*.

"These dinosaur characters are funny, fanciful, and silly. Children recognize the absurdities of adults in an instant—one of my favorite points of this story."

FOR PETER

THE BLUE SKY PRESS

For information regarding permission, please write to: Permissions Department,
The Blue Sky Press, an imprint of Scholastic Inc., 555 Broadway, New York, New York 10012.
The Blue Sky Press is a registered trademark of Scholastic Inc.
Library of Congress catalog card number: 98-31790
ISBN 0-590-38360-4
10 9 8 7 6 5 4 3 2 1   9/9 0/0 01 02 03
Printed in Singapore   46
First printing, September 1999
Production supervision by Angela Biola
Designed by Kathleen Westray